KU-764-504

HEAVE HO!

Pirates Can Work Together

Written by
Tom Easton

Illustrated by
Mike Gordon

WAYLAND

One hot day, on the *Golden Duck*,
Sam was hard at work in the galley,
making his speciality: Seven Seas Soup.

HEAVE HO!

Pirates Can Work Together

First published in 2015 by Wayland

Text © Wayland 2015
Illustrations© Mike Gordon

Wayland
Carmelite House
50 Victoria Embankment
London EC4Y 0DZ

Wayland Australia
Level 17/207 Kent Street
Sydney, NSW 2000

All rights reserved

Commissioning editor: Victoria Brooker
Creative design: Basement68

A catalogue record for this book is
available from the British Library.
Dewey number: 823.9'2-dc23

ISBN 978 0 7502 9584 0
Ebook ISBN 978 0 7502 9628 1

Printed in China

10 9 8 7 6 5 4 3 2 1

Wayland is a division of
Hachette Children's Group,
an Hachette UK company.
www.hachette.co.uk

"The Captain likes a little salt in his soup," Sam said to himself. "Though too much isn't good for you." So he added a small pinch. As the soup bubbled away, he went to help on deck.

"Get the mainsail down," the Captain shouted. "There's a storm coming."

Sam started winding the capstan. It was hard work.

"This is taking forever," the Captain said, as he watched Sam sweat. "You need help."

The Captain went below decks to find someone to help. As he passed the bubbling soup, he stopped. "Sam never puts enough salt in," he muttered, and added a pinch, but not too much!

8

Spying a foot poking out from behind
a barrel of pickled herring, the Captain went
to investigate. It was Davy, asleep as usual.
"WAKE UP!" the Captain roared.
"Sam needs help on deck."

Davy grumbled and slowly followed the Captain.
He did not want to help. He'd been having
a lovely dream about Sam's soup.

Licking his lips, he added a tiny pinch
of salt to the bubbling pot as he passed.
"Not too much," he thought to himself.

Sam hadn't got very far with the mainsail.
"Davy, you'd better start on the topsail,"
Captain Cod said, "or we'll be here all day."

Dark storm clouds approached.

The two sails inched down as the pirates heaved.

12

The Captain opened a hatch and shouted for Pete to come and help.

"PETE!"

As Pete walked through the galley he added some salt to the soup for the Captain.

"One pinch is enough," he thought.

"Get that mizzen down,"
the Captain roared as Pete came up on deck.
"These two lubbers are taking forever.
We need to work on all three sails."

Sam sweated, Davy dripped, Pete
perspired. Even poor Polly Parrot tried to help
by flapping her wings to keep the captain cool. But
still the sails weren't coming down quickly enough.

"NELL," Captain Cod roared.

"NELL!"

The delicious smell of the soup had brought
Nell into the galley when she heard the Captain
call for her. There wasn't time to taste it, but
she knew Sam never put enough salt in
so she added a tiny pinch.

"These useless pirates have muscles
like noodles," the Captain fumed.
"Even working on all three sails at once,
it's going to take too long. The ship will
capsize and we'll all drown!"

"Wouldn't it be better if we all worked
together on each sail?" Nell suggested.
The Captain thought this over.

"What are you doing, you fools?" he yelled.
"You should all be working TOGETHER!"

"But..." Pete said.
"Don't argue,"
the Captain bellowed.
"Just do it!"
"We should help too,"
Nell said to the Captain.
"What? Oh, yes, I suppose
so," the Captain said.

The pirates heaved and hoed.
Working together, the capstans turned
much more easily and the sails came
down quickly.

"I knew my muscles would make the difference," the Captain said, looking around proudly once the work was done.

The pirates were exhausted after their efforts and had a little rest.

Polly went off to check on the soup. She knew the Captain liked a bit of salt and added the tiniest of pinches.

Suddenly the storm broke, sending all the pirates rushing below decks. As the ship rocked safely, they all sat down to dinner and the Captain gave a speech. "Thanks to my quick thinking..." the Captain began.

"That's strange," everyone said.
"I only added a pinch."

NOTES FOR PARENTS AND TEACHERS

Pirates to the Rescue
The books in the 'Pirates to the Rescue' series are designed to help children recognise the virtues of good manners and behaviour. Reading these books will show children that their actions have a real effect on people around them, helping them to recognise what is right and wrong, and to think about what to do when faced with difficult choices.

Heave Ho!
'Heave Ho!' is intended to be an engaging and enjoyable read for children aged 4-7. The book will help children to recognise why it's okay to ask for help and that working as a team can often bring better results.

When Captain Cod instructs the pirates to each work on a different sail, he is encouraging them to work separately, which makes the task harder. Nell realises the Captain's mistake and communicates the solution. The Captain realises the sense of her suggestion and orders the pirates to begin working as a team. The task is then completed quickly and easily.

Meanwhile, below decks, the pirates are, individually, adding salt to the soup, each believing they are working to the common good. Here, it's a lack of communication that leads to an unpleasant surprise for them all.

Being able to work together with others as part of a team is not just a skill needed at school or within a family, it is a vital skill used in all areas of life.

Teamwork requires people to work co-operatively with others to achieve a common goal. For a team to work together effectively, it is important for all members to respect each other's abilities and opinions. Teamwork is a social activity and involves interaction and exchanging of ideas. Being a team member will help children to communicate with others.

30

Working as part of a team will strengthen social and emotional skills, help develop communication skills, and can improve confidence.

At school, children will have to work in pairs, or in smaller or larger groups, depending on the task. They will work in teams for sporting activities. Pupils will also tend to engage in unsupervised team activities at break times. Team activities can lead to competitiveness. Encourage children to be a good sport and a team player.

Suggested follow-up activities

Talk to your child about the events in the book. Why was it better that the pirates worked together in lowering the sails? How could the salty soup problem have been avoided?

Make a Seven Sea Soup at home with your child and other family members. Discuss beforehand what should be in the soup and let each member of the family add one or two ingredients. Eat the soup together and encourage everyone to describe how well the ingredients work together.

Children can really enjoy being part of a team, but being excluded can be upsetting. Explain to children the importance of not excluding anyone and how upsetting it can be to be left out.

Ask children to work together on a art team project. Paint a mural as a group on a large sheet of paper or an old sheet.

Ask children to put on a short play, or hold an obstacle relay race. Ensure everyone has a clear role and a job to do.

31

BOOKS TO SHARE

I Can Make a Difference: A First Look at Setting a Good Example
by Pat Thomas and Lesley Harker (Wayland, 2015)

This delightful picturebook helps children to understand
why it is important to have good manners and help others,
and how consideration for others can make working
and playing together more enjoyable for everyone.

Not Fair, Won't Share (Our Emotions)
by Sue Graves (Watts, 2011)

Miss Clover has made a space station. Posy, Ben and Alfie must take
turns to play with it. But Posy doesn't want to share, and everyone
gets cross. Can the children learn to work together and share?

Teamwork Isn't My Thing, and I Don't Like to Share
by Julia Cook (Boys Town Press, 2012)

RJ has a bad day. He doesn't want to work in
a group at school and has to share the last
biscuit with his sister. With help from his
mum, he learn how working as a team
and sharing can make him
feel happy.

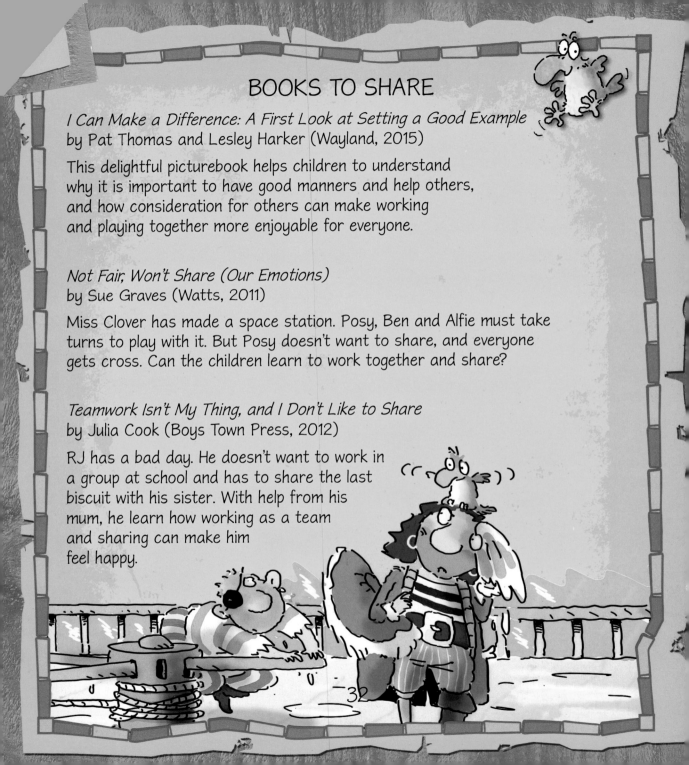

Read all the books in this series:

Ahoy There!:
Pirates Can Listen
978 0 7502 9585 7

Helping Polly Parrot!:
Pirates Can Be Kind
978 0 7502 8926 9

Aye Aye Captain!:
Pirates Can Be Polite
978 0 7502 8296 3

I Did It!:
Pirates Can Be Honest
978 0 7502 8925 2

Heave Ho!:
Pirates Can Work Together
978 0 7502 9584 0

Treasure Ahoy!:
Pirates Can Share
978 0 7502 8298 7